THE SEA DRAGONS
DRAGON GIRLS
Sofia the Lagoon Dragon
Maddy Mara

DRAGON GIRLS

Sofia the Lagoon Dragon

by Maddy Mara

Scholastic Inc.

Copyright © 2023 by Maddy Mara

Illustrations by Barbara Szepesi Szucs, copyright © 2023 by Scholastic Inc.

ISBN 978-1-338-87550-8

10 9 8 7 6 5 4 3 2 1   23 24 25 26 27

Printed in the U.S.A. 40

First printing 2023

Book design by Cassy Price

1

The last day of aquatics camp was here. The campers were celebrating by having a party at the nearby lagoon. Sofia curled her toes around the edge of the rock and looked around.

From the moment she arrived, Sofia could tell the lagoon was a special place. The water was surrounded by rocky cliffs and lush greenery.

It glittered like a precious jewel. There was an impressive waterfall that flowed over the rocks before tumbling into the lagoon. The camp counselors had decorated the tall palm trees with paper lanterns, making everything look truly magical. Best of all, to one side was a long table loaded with tasty things to eat and drink.

"Sofia! Coming for a swim before we eat?"

Sofia looked over. On the little beach were her cabinmates and new besties, Grace and Zoe. They waved at her. Sofia smiled and waved back.

Normally, it took her a little while to make

friends. But she had clicked instantly with Grace and Zoe. Maybe it was because they all loved water. Or maybe it was because they shared an amazing secret. The three girls had the ability to travel to a place called the Magic Forest. This was a beautiful land, ruled by the kindly Tree Queen. In the Magic Forest, Sofia and her friends were no longer normal girls. They became Sea Dragons! As Sea Dragons, they had powerful mermaid-like tails that helped them swim very fast underwater. They also had strong wings so they could fly high above the treetops.

Sofia loved how she could roar as a dragon. For a start, roaring was fun. But it was more than that. The Sea Dragons' roars had amazing magical powers!

But the Magic Forest was facing a terrible threat. There was an evil Fire Queen, who was trying to destroy the seas surrounding the forest. She had kidnapped three Sea Keepers, who were in charge of looking after the seas and keeping them in balance.

So far, Sofia, Grace, and Zoe had rescued two of the missing Sea Keepers: the dolphin leader and the sea turtle. Sofia couldn't wait to return and help rescue the third and final one.

"I'll be there in a sec," Sofia called to her friends. "I just want to do one dive."

Sofia loved diving. She had come to camp so she could work on her diving skills. She had learned a lot during the daily training sessions at the camp's dive pool. Just today, she had perfected her reverse dive. It had been so cool! She really wanted to try it out again.

The late-afternoon light was slowly turning the water from bright blue to purple. Low on the horizon, a full moon was rising. Sofia shivered with happiness. This was the perfect setting for a dive! Once again, she looked down. She had already checked with her dive instructor, Mel, that the lagoon was safe, and deep enough for diving. The water was so clear, she could see all the way down. The bottom of the lagoon was strewn with smooth pebbles that glimmered like treasure.

I'll dive down there and scoop one up, Sofia decided.

As she prepared herself to dive, she heard something. It was a song. At first Sofia thought one of the kids down below was singing. Or perhaps the counselors were playing music?

Magic Forest, Magic Forest, come explore...

Then Sofia smiled. She had heard this song twice before and knew what it meant. She was going to return to the Magic Forest! She looked at the bracelet on her wrist. On the silver chain hung a white, fan-shaped shell. The Tree Queen had given it to her the first time she and her friends had visited the Magic Forest. Grace and Zoe had bracelets just like it.

Right now, Sofia's shell was glowing pale pink. Excitement bubbled inside her, but she kept her breath steady and her mind focused. She ran through the steps of the dive in her head, making sure she had them straight. As she did so, she heard the song, louder than before.

Magic Forest, Magic Forest, come explore.

"Don't worry, Magic Forest. I'm coming!" Sofia murmured.

With a last steadying breath, she jumped up into the air. The colors of the lagoon swirled by in a blur as she somersaulted backward. Sofia plunged through the lagoon's glassy surface. Cool water rushed past her as she dove down to the lagoon bed. As she dove, the water seemed to change. It felt softer somehow. Then, as Sofia reached out for a gleaming stone, she heard the last line of the song.

Magic Forest, Magic Forest, hear my roar!

Grabbing the stone, Sofia began swimming back to the surface. Above her, through the water, Sofia could see the wobbly outline of the full moon. It had a shimmery, silvery-pink glow to it. Sofia kicked hard, swimming up with all her might.

Bursting through the surface, she took a big gulp of air and looked around. A huge smile crept over her face. Just as she had expected, everything had changed!

2

Actually, not *everything* had changed. Sofia

was still in a beautiful lagoon with a powerful

waterfall cascading over the rocks. There was

still a small beach strewn with delicate shells.

And there was still a full moon, hanging low

in the sky.

But other things were very different. All those

excited kids, chatting and laughing on their last day of camp, had vanished. Everything was silent, except for the birds singing. It was different from the birdsong she was used to back home. These birds tinkled and chimed like little bells.

There was a different scent wafting in the air, too. Sofia could no longer smell the goodies the counselors had prepared for their party. Now there was the aroma of tropical fruit and just the faintest hint of hot chocolate.

The biggest change of all was in Sofia herself. Her legs had been replaced by a beautiful coral-pink mermaid's tail. On her back grew flowing, tendril-like wings. She was entirely covered with gleaming scales, and she had a set of impressive talons on each paw.

But what about her roar? Could she still do that? There was only one way to find out! Sofia filled her lungs with air, then roared with all her might. The sound burst out of her, bouncing off the surrounding cliffs in a satisfying echo. It sounded like there were a hundred Dragon Girls in the lagoon, not just one!

Sofia felt something bump against her. Looking down, she saw a tiny pink jellyfish. Sofia had seen lots of jellyfish before. But she'd never seen one with friendly eyes and a big smile!

The jellyfish clapped two tentacles. "Nice roaring!"

"Thanks," said Sofia. It was funny how normal it felt to talk to creatures here in the Magic Forest. "I'm Sofia, by the way."

The little jellyfish did a twirl, fanning herself out like a dancer. "I am JellyJo," she replied. "The Tree Queen sent me here to fetch you.

She needs to speak to you and your friends urgently."

Sofia nodded. "We must rescue the third Sea Keeper."

"That's right," JellyJo said, sounding serious. "And the Fire Queen is determined to stop you. The Magic Forest and our seas are swarming with her Fire Sparks. They are bigger than ever."

Sofia's heart sank at this. She did not like the Fire Sparks! They stung when they touched you. If they had grown bigger, that probably meant their stings would be worse.

I won't let it worry me, Sofia told herself.

Sofia knew that the Fire Queen had a terrible

plan in mind. She was determined to destroy the seas that surrounded the Magic Forest. But Sofia and her friends were just as determined to stop her!

JellyJo pulsed up and down. Then, to Sofia's surprise, the jellyfish rose out of the water and into the air.

"Let's go, Sofia!" she called, beckoning her with several tentacles.

"Coming," Sofia replied. With a strong flap of her wings, she followed JellyJo into the warm evening air.

Sofia was sorry to leave the lovely lagoon. But she knew that she and her friends had an important job to do.

Sofia flew across the lagoon behind JellyJo, who was surprisingly fast! At the far edge was the Magic Forest itself, filled with mysterious smells and sounds. The air cooled as Sofia and JellyJo weaved their way through the tall trees. The deeper they flew, the darker and quieter the forest became.

After a little while, Sofia started to feel strange. Her thoughts were swirling. She knew she was in the Magic Forest, but where was she heading again? And why?

Sofia knew this feeling. She always got confused when the Fire Sparks were attacking. But there were no Fire Sparks nearby. What was going on? Sofia's unease grew.

Then, through the trees, Sofia saw something glowing.

We're at the glade already! she thought with relief.

The glade was where the Tree Queen lived. It was protected by powerful magic. Sofia knew she would be safe there.

But as they flew closer, Sofia gasped. The glow was not coming from the glade at all. Instead, she saw a whirling mass of Fire Sparks. It was like a huge bonfire. Worse, each spark was much bigger than when Sofia had last been in the Magic Forest. JellyJo was right! Their buzzing was louder, too.

"Watch out!" cried JellyJo, shaking like Jell-O.

The glowing, buzzing mass rose into the air and swarmed close to Sofia and JellyJo. Sofia swerved to the right and sped up, her heart pounding. She was flying as fast as she could after JellyJo. But the sound of the buzzing behind them grew anyway. To make things even harder, the fogginess in Sofia's head was building.

Weaving between the trunks was slowing her down. *We need to get above the treetops,* decided Sofia.

"Good idea," whispered JellyJo. "Let's do it."

With a jolt of surprise, Sofia realized JellyJo could understand her thoughts. How magical! Together, they whooshed through the canopy of the Magic Forest and up into the early evening sky. The clouds were turning gorgeous shades of pink and purple. But there was no time to enjoy the view. Sofia knew the sparks were not far behind.

Sure enough, the glowing mass streaked out of the forest and into the air a moment later. Luckily, up here it was easier to fly fast. Finally, Sofia managed to get far ahead of the annoying creatures. For now, at least.

"Look down there." JellyJo pointed a tentacle.

Sofia saw another glow between the trees below. For a horrible moment Sofia thought it was yet more Fire Sparks.

But no! This time it really was the welcoming

light of the glade. Sofia flew until she was directly over the force field around the glade. She had dived from some very high places before. But she'd never dived from this height. And she'd certainly never dived into a glade! On the other hand, it was definitely the quickest way to the Tree Queen. It was also the most fun.

"Can I do it?" she wondered aloud.

"Of course you can!" said JellyJo, waving all her tentacles at once. "I must go, but I will be back whenever you need me. Now, let's see you dive!"

3

Sofia hovered a moment longer, looking at the force field below. She breathed deeply, focusing her mind. Then she tucked her wings by her sides, stretched out her front paws, and started free-falling. What would it feel like to dive through the force field? She really hoped that it wouldn't be like a trampoline and bounce her back into the air!

With a flick of her tail, Sofia sped up. The colors of the forest flashed by. The glade's forcefield loomed larger and larger until suddenly, it was right there in front of her! Sofia's scales tingled as she passed right through the glowing shield. Phew! Diving through the force field had gone really well. But there was one thing she hadn't thought about: how to finish the dive!

Luckily, there was a pond in the glade's center. It wasn't very big, but it would have to do. Sofia stretched out her wings to slow herself down, then tucked them back in and managed to dive directly into the pond. Quickly, she did a somersault and headed straight back up to the surface.

As she burst out of the pond and into the air, Sofia saw Grace and Zoe hovering nearby. They were both dripping with water.

"Hi! Why are you two wet?" Sofia asked. "Has it been raining?"

Grace and Zoe started laughing. "We're wet from the splash you just made when you dove into the pond!"

"Oops," Sofia said. "Sorry!"

"That's okay," Grace said. "It was quite nice. Like being caught in a summer rainstorm."

Zoe flew over to the lush tree in the center of the glade. "Come on, you two! The Tree Queen is about to change."

The tree was swaying gently from side to side. Sofia watched in awe as it transformed into the elegant figure of the Tree Queen, dressed in her flowing green robes. Sofia had seen this transformation twice before already, but it still took her breath away. The Magic Forest truly was, well, magical!

The Tree Queen smiled at the Sea Dragons. But could Sofia see a hint of worry on her welcoming face?

"I am so glad you are back," the Tree Queen said warmly. "You three have already done so much for our seas."

Sofia felt a flush of pride. It was true that she and her friends had had some big adventures here. While they were rescuing the dolphin and the turtle, they had encountered Shiver Sharks, a lovely group of baby turtles, and some very relaxed surfing seals. Plus, they had battled with lots of Fire Sparks and, of course, the Fire Queen herself. So far, the Sea Dragons had managed to deal with everything.

But Sofia felt a little nervous. Who knew what lay ahead of them this time?

The Tree Queen seemed to sense Sofia's feelings. She looked at Sofia, her leaves rustling gently. "This last part of the quest won't be easy," she said softly. "The Fire Queen is extremely angry that you three have outsmarted her so far. And her Fire Sparks are bigger than ever, fueled by her fury."

Sofia nodded. "I saw them on the way here. They are huge!"

"Not only that, but the last of the Sea

Keepers—the narwhal Nara—is the most important of the trio. You must find her."

Despite the seriousness of the situation, Sofia couldn't help feeling pleased. Narwhals were her favorite sea creature. Maybe she would actually get to meet one!

"Why is the narwhal so important?" Zoe asked.

"All three Sea Keepers must be in the Undersea Garden for the winding ceremony," explained the Tree Queen. "But it is the narwhal who actually winds the Water Watch."

"The Water Watch keeps the seas healthy, right?" Grace said. "It makes the tides ebb and flow, and keeps the water at the right level."

"Exactly," said the Tree Queen. "Once a year it must be wound. And that day is today."

"Today!" Sofia gasped, summing up how all three Dragon Girls felt. "Will we have time?"

The Tree Queen looked at her, her brown eyes very serious indeed. "There is no doubt that it will be challenging," she said. "The Fire Queen will do everything she can to stop you. But the welfare of the Magic Forest's seas depends on you succeeding."

A mix of emotions swirled inside Sofia. She wanted to help more than anything. But it all sounded very hard!

She felt someone squeeze her right paw. It was Grace, smiling at her. Then someone squeezed the other paw. That was Zoe.

"We're going to do this," Zoe said firmly.

"Together," Grace added.

Sofia's nerves instantly disappeared. Her friends were right! Sure, this quest was going to be a big challenge. Their biggest yet. But somehow, it did not seem nearly so scary knowing that her friends would be by her side.

"That's the spirit, Sofia," the Tree Queen said softly. Like always, it was as if the Tree Queen could read Sofia's mind.

"Your Majesty, where should we start looking for the narwhal?" Sofia asked quickly. She could see that the queen was starting to turn back into a tree.

"I suggest you start by finding the smart fish," the queen said, her voice already growing faint. "They will help you."

"The smart fish?" Sofia repeated. *What does that mean?*

But there was no time to find out. With a final rustling of leaves, the Tree Queen was once more a tree.

4

"Any ideas on where we might find...um, smart fish?" Zoe asked.

"No ideas whatsoever," Grace admitted with a shrug.

Sofia was about to say that unfortunately she didn't know, either, when she felt a gentle tugging on her paw. Her bracelet! The shell was glowing.

Zoe also noticed it. "Looks like you're the one to guide us this time, Sofia!" she said. "Listen to the shell. It will tell you where to go."

Sofia brought the shell to her ear. A small voice began to speak. "The smart fish live in the lagoon. I will guide you there." Sofia had often listened to shells at the beach. But she had never heard a voice coming from one before!

Sofia flapped her wings and began heading for the glade's protective barrier. "Follow me!" she called to her friends. "We're going to the lagoon."

Soon the three Sea Dragons were back in the Magic Forest, winding through the thick foliage. Sofia kept an eye out for Fire Sparks. She had a feeling they were lurking close, watching them. Luckily, none appeared.

The shell did as it had promised, and before long Sofia, Grace, and Zoe were at the lagoon where Sofia had first arrived.

"Wow!" Grace breathed. "This place is amazing."

"Magical," Zoe agreed.

Sofia hovered on the spot and looked around. She was happy her friends loved the lagoon as much as she did. And the lagoon looked even better than it had before. The light from the setting sun struck the tall cliffs, making them shine like gold. The water swirled with bright pinks, rich purples, and refreshing blues. The waterfall looked as though it was made from crystal, the water tinkling like musical notes as it flowed down.

Sofia smiled. Her friends were right: This was clearly a magical place.

"Hey, what was that?" Grace pointed to the middle of the lagoon. "Something jumped out."

"I didn't see any—" Sofia started to say.

But as she spoke, a flash of neon leapt out of the water. As it came back down, it belly flopped onto the surface with a loud *THWACK!* A moment later, there were many more flashes.

"They're little fish!" exclaimed Zoe. "Maybe they're the ones we're looking for?"

Sofia nodded. "Could be. Let's go over and find out." She was curious to discover what they were doing. The belly flops looked painful.

The Sea Dragons flew over the water until they were directly above the leaping fish.

"Excuse me, are you the smart fish?" Sofia called.

But the fish did not seem to hear her.

"Maybe it's easier if we dive in and speak to them underwater," Grace suggested.

"Good idea," Zoe said.

She and Grace promptly dove into the water. Sofia dove, too, but she couldn't resist doing a quick somersault on her way down. She plunged through the smooth surface of the water, feeling the bubbles against her scales. The moment she came to a stop, she found herself surrounded by little shimmery fish!

"That was a great dive," one of them said.

"Can you teach us?" another fish asked eagerly. "We've been trying to teach ourselves, but we can't get it right."

For a moment, Sofia was too surprised to

speak. She had never been asked to teach a fish how to dive before!

"She can teach you," Zoe said, swimming over, "but first, we have a question. Are you the smart fish?"

The fish swished their glimmering tails. "We are!" they said proudly. "We are very, very smart. And that's why we must learn how to dive."

Grace frowned. "Why does being smart mean you must learn how to dive?"

"We are still in school," explained one of the little creatures.

"Don't most fish swim in schools?" Sofia asked. It was all very puzzling.

The fish swished their tails again. "Yes, but we want to be in college! And to get into Lagoon College, you have to pass a diving test. We might be smart, but we're no good at diving."

Zoe gave Sofia a look. "Do you think you can teach them?" she asked in a low voice. "I only said yes because I was hoping they'd help us with our quest. But I'm not sure how hard it will be."

Sofia shrugged. "I'm happy to try!"

It turned out that the smart fish were very good students. They listened carefully as Sofia explained why they kept belly flopping. A few of them even pulled out tiny notepads and pens and took notes.

"You need to arch your backs more as you curve toward the water," Sofia said, giving the fish a little demonstration.

The little fish nodded enthusiastically. Then they tried it out.

"Better," Sofia said encouragingly. "But swish your tails harder as you leap. You need to get higher so you can enter the water at the cor-rect angle."

This time, the smart fish all dove perfectly! After they'd each had a turn, they lined up in two rows.

"You are such a great diving teacher!" they said, beginning to swim away. "Now we must go. It's almost time for our next class. We like to be early. Thanks again!"

"Wait a minute, please?" Sofia asked. "We actually need your help! It's a question."

The fish clustered back around Sofia. "Ooh! We love questions! Is it a difficult one?"

"It's pretty difficult," Grace said.

"And it's also very important," Zoe added.

"What is it? What is it?" the fish asked eagerly. "We'll do our best!"

Sofia looked all around before speaking. This would be a very bad time to be attacked by Fire Sparks. "We're looking for the narwhal

Sea Keeper," she said in a low voice. "She has been taken by the Fire Queen. It's urgent that we find her before the full moon rises and the Water Watch needs winding. Do you have any idea where she might be?"

This time the smart fish moved their tails in a slow, sad way. "We don't know the answer to your question." Then their tail swishes got happier again. "But we know someone who might be able to help! He's the missing narwhal's best friend. Unfortunately, his home is very hard to find."

"But I bet a bunch of smart fish like you know the way, right?" Zoe asked, looking hopeful.

"Of course we do," said the fish. "But our next class starts soon. We don't have time."

The Sea Dragons looked at one another. They didn't want to make these smart fish late for class. But it was so important that they find the missing Sea Keeper. If they didn't, the whole lagoon might be drained!

The little fish looked at one another as well. Sofia got the feeling they could communicate without speaking.

Suddenly, the fish re-formed into their two neat lines. "We will take you part of the way. Get ready, though. We'll be going fast!"

5

The little fish shot off, their tails swishing so fast they were a blur. It was hard for Sofia and Zoe to keep up! Grace was an amazing swimmer, so she had no problems.

As well as being fast, the fish were very nimble. They darted this way and that, through floaty strands of seaweed and under coral arches. For the Sea Dragons, it was much harder to twist and turn. They were so much bigger! But they did their best.

We can't let them out of our sight! Sofia reminded herself, swimming as hard as she could.

Grace slowed down so Sofia could catch up with her. "Am I imagining it, or are we going deeper and deeper?"

"I wondered that, too," said Zoe, coming up on Sofia's other side. "I can feel a pressure in my ears."

Now that Zoe mentioned it, Sofia noticed her ears did feel different, too. Also, it was becoming harder to see in the dark water. But were they actually going down? Maybe they were going up? Sofia felt her pulse begin to beat faster. Uh-oh! She was starting to feel confused and foggy. That could only mean one thing . . .

"Watch out!" cried the school of fish from up ahead. "We're under attack!"

In the darkness, a glow had appeared. It was growing bigger and brighter by the second.

"Quick! Move into defense mode!" the little fish called to one another.

Swishing their tails furiously, the fish changed from two lines to one big mass. Sofia watched them in fascination. Were they try-ing to look like one giant fish? It was a pretty weird-looking one, if so. But maybe she was just too confused to see it clearly?

As the Fire Sparks drew closer, Sofia felt less sure about everything. And was it possible that the sparks were even bigger than last time?

"They're not forming a giant fish," said a familiar voice.

Sofia turned. With a jolt of happiness, she saw that JellyJo was back.

"They're forming a giant Fire Spark," JellyJo explained.

JellyJo was right! The group of little fish looked exactly like an enormous Fire Spark. Only the fish spark was bright silver instead of fiery gold.

Rather than swimming away from the sparks, the fish sped toward them. It was amazing to watch them move as one. The sparks buzzed with anger and began zigzagging here and there to get away from the giant fish spark. The dark water was soon streaked with light and crackling electricity.

"You should do the same as the fish," JellyJo

urged Sofia, bobbing close by. "You're stronger when you stick together!"

Sofia nodded. She and her friends were definitely more powerful when they joined forces. Looking around, she could just make out the shapes of Zoe and Grace in the dark waters. In the flashes of light from the Fire Sparks, Sofia glimpsed her friends bravely battling them. But Sofia could see that they were struggling.

Quickly, she swam over to her friends and grabbed hold of them, pulling them close. She wrapped one wing around Grace and the other around Zoe. Having her friends right there made her feel better at once.

"We're strong on our own," she reminded

her friends. "But together, we're unbeatable. So shall we roar?"

Zoe and Grace didn't need to answer. Instead, they opened their mouths and roared as loudly as they could. Seeing the waters swirl and churn with their sea-powered roars made Sofia feel more confident than ever. She added her roar to the mix.

The Fire Sparks crackled and swooshed, but the Sea Dragons' roars pushed them back. The sparks tried to swim around their roars, but the giant fishy spark blocked their way.

Finally, with an angry buzz, the Fire Sparks gave up and disappeared back into the watery depths.

Sofia and her friends grinned at one another.

"High tail!" Sofia said.

She, Zoe, and Grace turned around and clapped their mermaid-like tails together.

"You did it!" JellyJo cried, clapping her tentacles. Then she began drifting away. "I'll be back if you need me!" she called.

The school of fish separated and re-formed two lines. They swam over. "Well done, Sea Dragons!" they said. "Your roars got rid of those nasty creatures."

"Thanks! And well done to you all," Sofia said. "It was very brainy of you to form one big shape like that."

The fish flipped their tails in a pleased sort of way. "We decided to fight fire with fire," they explained. "That trick doesn't always work. But this time it did! Now we must hurry to class."

Sofia looked at them in dismay. "But what about taking us to the narwhal's best friend? How will we know which way to go?"

"Look behind you," the fish replied together.

Sofia turned. There, just visible in the darkness, was a gateway. The gate itself was a huge, polished clamshell.

"That is the entrance to the Narwhal Kingdom," the little fish explained. "If you follow the main path, you shouldn't have a problem finding the house."

Sofia nodded. "Thanks so much! And I am sure we can ask the narwhals who live in the kingdom for directions if we have trouble finding it."

The fish gently swayed their tails, considering what Sofia had said. "Well, you could try that," they said, sounding doubtful. "But that might not end up being very helpful."

"Why not?" Zoe asked. "Are the narwhals unfriendly?"

Sofia hoped this wasn't the case. She loved narwhals!

"Quite the opposite," the fish said. "Narwhals are extremely friendly. And they love to help. They're just..."

"They're just what?" Grace prompted.

The little fish looked at one another. "Let's just say that there aren't any narwhal schools," they said eventually. "We must go! It was a pleasure meeting you, Sea Dragons. We hope you succeed in your quest."

In their perfect lines, the fish turned and swam away.

The Sea Dragons waved them off. "They were the smartest fish I have ever spoken to," Zoe said, her voice full of admiration.

"Same," Sofia said. Then she laughed. "But they are also the ONLY fish I've ever spoken to. Now, are we ready? Let's go meet some narwhals!"

6

As the little group approached the gate, a narwhal swam up from the other side. It was pale purple, with a long twirly horn. It stuck its horn through the bars of the gate and stared at the Sea Dragons suspiciously.

"What kind of fish are you?" the narwhal asked.

"We're not fish at all," Sofia explained. "We're Sea Dragons."

The narwhal narrowed his eyes. "Are you sure you're not those nasty hot fish that have been swimming around here lately? You don't look the same, but maybe you are in disguise."

"We're definitely not Fire Sparks," Grace assured him.

"Good. But even so, we're not letting in any strangers," the narwhal said. "One of our community, Nara, has gone missing, and we're all very, very upset!" The narwhal's voice quivered.

"We're actually here to help find her," Zoe explained.

"Well, in that case, what are you waiting for? Come right in!" the narwhal said brightly.

"Maybe you could open the gate?" Sofia asked politely.

"Of course! Silly me," the narwhal said.

He tried to swim to the left but had clearly forgotten his long horn was sticking through the bars of the gate and clunked it against a rail. Then he swam to the right and clunked it against a different rail. The Sea Dragons tried not to laugh. Finally, the narwhal swam backward and managed to undo the gate's latch with his horn.

"Welcome to the Narwhal Kingdom! I'm Toothy," he said as the gate swung open. "Where can I take you?"

"We're looking for the best friend of the narwhal who disappeared," Sofia said. "Can you take us to his house?"

"No problem," Toothy said. "Follow me."

Toothy tossed his head, slicing through some nearby seaweed strands with his horn. Then he swam off down a pathway lined with tall columns. The Sea Dragons quickly fell in behind him, swishing their tails to keep up.

On either side of the path were elegant buildings. They all seemed to be made from mother-of-pearl, and each had an extremely pointed roof.

"This is a very grand kingdom," Zoe commented as they swam.

"It's also a very pointy kingdom!" Grace added.

Sofia couldn't help noticing that there were lots of scratches and holes in the beautiful buildings. She got the feeling that narwhals often forgot they had superlong horns stuck to their foreheads.

"Where are all the narwhals?" Zoe asked Toothy. "Your kingdom is deserted."

"And what's that sound?" Grace asked.

There was a wailing, moaning noise coming from some of the buildings.

"That is the sound of narwhals crying," Toothy explained, his voice trembling again. "Since Nara was taken, we've been beside ourselves. We narwhals are very close. Many of us haven't left our homes for days."

"Don't worry," Sofia said kindly. She hated the idea of a whole kingdom being sad, especially a narwhal one. "We will find her."

"I am so relieved to hear that," Toothy said,

and Sofia had to jump out of the way of Toothy's horn as he swung around to give her a grateful look. "And here we are. This is where Nara's best friend lives."

Sofia looked up and gasped. The building was spectacular! Instead of having one or two pointy towers like many of the other narwhal buildings they'd passed, this one had countless towers. And each one was topped with gold. A little way off were several burly-looking narwhals, guarding what appeared to be the entrance.

"This looks like a palace!" Grace remarked.

"That's because it *is* a palace," Toothy said.

Grace just managed to somersault away from Toothy's horn as he turned to her. "Princes always live in palaces, don't they?"

"Yes, but hang on," Zoe said. "Are you saying that Nara's best friend is the prince of the Narwhal Kingdom? Why didn't you tell us?"

"You didn't ask!" Toothy said. "Come on, let's go inside."

Sofia stared at the narwhal in surprise. "We can't just walk into Narwhal Palace," she reminded Toothy. "There are guards out front, for one thing."

"Silly Sea Dragons! We can go inside," Toothy said, swimming toward the entrance. "I think I'm allowed inside my own home."

As Sofia and her friends watched, the guards bowed to Toothy, their horns accidentally clunking together.

"Greetings, Your Royal Toothiness," they murmured.

"I guess another thing we didn't ask is, *Are you the prince we're looking for?*" Zoe said, shaking her head.

But Toothy had already swum past the guards and didn't hear her.

"It seems so." Sofia shrugged. "We'd better keep up with him!"

Quickly, the three Sea Dragons passed the guards, who were too busy trying to untangle their horns to pay them any attention.

Within moments they were inside the pointy palace. It was in chaos! Narwhals swam this way and that, weeping, yelling, or talking at the tops of their voices.

Sofia could hardly bear to watch. She kept expecting them to crash into one another—and often they did! There were horn scratches and holes on the palace walls. There was even a deep crack in the floor.

Sofia frowned at it. Surely a narwhal horn hadn't made that crack?

"What's going on?" Grace wondered.

"We are organizing a search party for Nara," Prince Toothy explained, swimming over. "But it is very difficult. We narwhals are good at organizing other kinds of parties. But search parties seem to be a bit trickier."

Sofia swam as close to Prince Toothy as she could while keeping an eye on his horn. "Don't forget, we are here to help you," she said.

Toothy's eyes filled with tears, which mingled

with the swirling ocean water. "Thank you, Sea Dragons. It has been hard to be in my palace since Nara was taken. It all happened right here, in fact. If only I could have stopped those hot fish in time!" Toothy began to howl.

Sofia's mind whirled. "Nara was taken from this room?"

"Yes," Toothy sobbed. "Those horrible burning fish broke through the floor! They were so bright that I was forced to close my eyes. And when I opened them again, Nara was gone."

Sofia swam over to the huge crack in the floor. The edges of it looked like they'd been burned. Glancing down, she could see a faint glow through the crack.

"The sparks must have taken Nara down there," Sofia said.

The good news was that Sofia was pretty sure where Nara had gone. The bad news was that they would have to dive down there themselves to rescue her.

7

Grace and Zoe approached Sofia and peered into the crack.

"I get the feeling you're planning to dive down there," Grace said.

Sofia nodded. "It's clearly where the Fire Sparks took Nara," she pointed out. As she spoke, the shell on her bracelet began to glow.

Sofia held it up to show her friends. "Even the shell is saying it's the right direction."

"Okay, then! Let's go," Zoe said, trying to sound brave.

"We'll come, too," Toothy said, slapping his fins against his side to get the others' attention. "Come on, everyone. Let's follow these Sea Dragons!"

Instantly, all the narwhals surged at the crack in the palace floor, getting tangled up in a scrum of horns, flippers, and tails.

The Sea Dragons had to gently pull them apart by their tails and then calm them down.

Once the narwhals were all free again, Sofia came up with a plan. "I will dive first," she announced to the group. "And if it's safe, then the rest of you can follow."

Sofia knew that she was the best diver out of her friends, and while the narwhals meant well, they seemed very accident-prone.

Sofia wanted to get down there as quickly as possible. And she definitely didn't want to get tangled in any narwhal horns along the way!

Zoe nodded. "Yes, you go on ahead. We'll come as soon as we can with the narwhals."

Grace sighed. "I don't like splitting up, but I can see it's the best thing to do."

Sofia took a deep breath and focused her thoughts. Then, before her nerves got the better of her, she dove through the crack.

The dark, cold seawater swirled around her. As she got farther away from the palace, Sofia felt more and more alone. Just as this thought entered her mind, JellyJo appeared! And this time, she was glowing with a gentle pink light. It was very handy!

"You're not alone, Sofia," JellyJo said. "I'm here with you—to keep you company and to light your way."

Sofia felt instantly better.

At first, the gap they were swimming through was very narrow. At some points, Sofia had to tuck in her wings to squeeze between sharp rocks. But luckily, JellyJo was by her side,

lighting up the area and showing her where the dangers lay.

Gradually, the gap grew wider and wider until it opened up completely.

The strange light that Sofia had spotted from up in Narwhal Palace grew brighter.

Soon three giant shapes loomed up from the gloomy seabed.

As Sofia got closer, she saw that there were three clamshells on the bottom of the ocean floor. They were huge—almost as big as Sofia herself. And each one emitted a strange blue-green light.

"What is this place?" Sofia wondered aloud, looking around.

"We're in the Undersea," explained JellyJo, pulsing beside her. "It's a vast ocean that runs below the one we were just in. It's where the Undersea Garden is found."

Sofia's heart leapt. "The Undersea Garden! Isn't that where the Water Watch is?"

"It is," JellyJo said. "It is very close, in fact. Very close, but also very far."

Sofia turned to JellyJo. "What do you mean?"

But before JellyJo could explain, a new light suddenly appeared. Unlike the cool bluish light of the giant clams, or JellyJo's gentle pink glow, this light was unbearable. It was so bright and hot!

The figure of a tall woman appeared. She was draped in a dress made of fire, and her flaming hair crackled with electricity, even though they were all deep underwater.

Sofia instantly knew who it was. She gasped. "The Fire Queen!"

"Very good, Sea Dragon," the Fire Queen sneered. "You're clearly smarter than those

bumbling narwhals. But that is not saying very much."

Anger burbled inside Sofia. The queen had caused so many problems for the seas. She even wanted to destroy them! And now she was being rude about the narwhals, who had never harmed anyone.

But Sofia was feeling something else, too. A wash of confusion. It was the same feeling she got when the Fire Sparks were close, but this was far more intense.

"Just breathe deeply, and don't let her upset you," JellyJo murmured. "Focus, like you do when you are about to dive."

Sofia did as she suggested and felt some of the fogginess lift.

The Fire Queen was watching Sofia intently. Her dark eyes glimmered and her hair rose and fell with the movement of the water. "Perhaps you're no smarter than the narwhals after all," she mused. "How about we do a little test to find out?"

Sofia felt her stomach tighten. "What do you mean, a test?"

The Fire Queen swished her long, flaming skirts as she floated up above the three clamshells.

"The narwhal you are so busily looking for is trapped inside one of these shells," said the Fire Queen, her voice crackling with hot menace. "If you can guess correctly which one, I will let her go. But be warned! One of the other shells is full of my trusty sparks. You might have noticed that I have been creating some very large specimens lately? These are my largest, most powerful ones yet. And they will be delighted to come out and meet you."

Sofia gulped. "And in the third shell?" she asked. She was doing her best to keep her breath slow and steady. But she could feel the confusion and worry taking hold of her thoughts again. "What is in that one?"

The Fire Queen's flames flared brighter as she smiled a nasty, gleaming smile. "I've kept that one empty. It's just the right size for a Sea Dragon, don't you think?"

Sofia glared at the Fire Queen. Inside, her heart was beating very fast. But there was no way she was going to show the Fire Queen how worried she was!

The Fire Queen stretched out her hands, pointing to the three clamshells below.

"So, Sea Dragon," she said. "Here's the burning question: Which shell do you choose?"

8

Sofia looked from one shell to the other, think-ing hard. They all looked pretty much the same. How could she possibly choose? Then she had an idea. The clamshell with the Fire Sparks inside would surely be very warm. If she touched the shells, she could narrow her choice down to only two!

She reached out a paw toward the clam-shells, but the Fire Queen swooped in to block her. "No cheating, Sea Dragon!" she hissed.

Another wave of confusion washed over Sofia. What was she looking for again? For some reason, Sofia found herself drawn to the clamshell in the middle. Was something in there? She shook her head, trying to clear the fog from it.

JellyJo swam up close. "Remember, you're looking for the missing narwhal. She is inside one of these shells."

That's right! thought Sofia, *I'm looking for the missing Sea Keeper.* For the millionth time she was grateful that JellyJo was there to help.

But still, she really wished she could talk to Grace and Zoe.

Once again, Sofia found herself looking at the middle shell. Was this the one with the missing narwhal inside? If only there were a way to tell!

The Fire Queen swirled around above her. "Hurry up, Sea Dragon! I haven't got all day. Choose a clamshell or I will choose one for you!" she demanded.

The Fire Queen seemed to be getting brighter and hotter, making the water uncomfortably warm.

"Just tune her out," JellyJo urged.

Yes! Sofia needed to treat the Fire Queen

like the crowd at a diving competition. She

would block out the queen and concentrate on

her own breathing. Sofia took deep breaths as

she looked from one shell to another. It really

was an impossible decision. She was just going

to have to pick one!

"I choose—" she started to say.

But she was interrupted by a huge racket.

There were lots of clinking noises, like some-one rifling through a cutlery drawer. There were also cries of "Ouch!" and "Oops, sorry!" and "Hang on, I'm stuck..."

Sofia whirled around to see a most remark-able sight. Diving down toward them was a cluster of narwhals, Prince Toothy leading the way. And on either side of him were Zoe and Grace!

The Fire Queen shot up high in the water, heat and light streaming from her. "What are you all doing here?" she muttered angrily. "Ah, but you have no idea, do you?" She grinned.

As the queen said that, Sofia felt the famil-iar waves of confusion heading her way. But now that her friends were here, it was different. The muddled feeling washed over her and then simply floated away.

Sofia called to Zoe and Grace. "The narwhal is inside one of those giant clamshells," she explained. "I can only choose one. For some reason I think it's the middle one. What do you think?"

"We trust you, Sofia," Grace said simply.

Zoe nodded. "Totally," she agreed. "You've got to follow your instincts."

The pod of narwhals crowded around. "We think you should trust your gut, too," Toothy said.

Sofia felt a warm glow inside. It was so good to know that she was supported like this. She turned to face the Fire Queen. "I choose the middle shell," she said firmly.

The Fire Queen swished down until she was hovering over the three shells. A curious light burned in her eyes. Sofia did not like the look of it one bit!

"You are correct, Sea Dragon," she said slowly. "The narwhal is indeed in that one." The queen pressed on the shell.

It sprang open, and out swam a narwhal. The narwhal looked around in astonishment at the crowd. "What's going on?"

"Nara!" Toothy cried. He tried to swim toward his friend, but the Fire Queen blocked his path.

"You don't seriously believe that I would let

you take her, do you?" She laughed nastily. "As if I would let anything get in the way of destroying these horrible, waste-of-space seas!"

Sofia remained very still, watching to see what the Fire Queen would do next. Whatever it was, Sofia knew it would be sneaky. She tried to stay calm, but her mind was racing. "We are stronger and smarter than you think," Sofia insisted, turning to her friends to include them.

"Are you *really*?" the Fire Queen asked sarcastically. "Perhaps this will change your mind."

With that, she darted over to the clamshell on the left and opened it. Instantly, the water swarmed with huge, buzzing Fire Sparks. They charged at the Sea Dragons and the narwhals, filling the water with heat and the sound of their buzzing.

Then the Fire Queen opened the clam on the right. Yet more Fire Sparks swam out!

"That's right, I lied!" The queen cackled as the second batch of sparks zipped about. "TWO of the shells contained my trusty helpers. And look! Now I have three empty shells, just waiting to trap three Sea Dragons."

Sofia swished her tail, batting the huge Fire Sparks out of her way. When Sofia had first met the Fire Queen, she had been scared. But Sofia no longer felt afraid—she didn't even feel angry. She just felt really, really determined to stop her.

"That's just not going to happen," Sofia said in a calm voice.

Zoe and Grace swam up beside her. "It absolutely isn't," they agreed, sounding every bit as sure as Sofia.

"Ha!" the Fire Queen sneered. "Then what IS going to happen?"

"This!" Sofia said.

Together, the three friends opened their jaws and roared. They had done some pretty impressive roars during this adventure. But these were the loudest, strongest, and most sea-roaring-est roars of all!

9

While she roared with her friends, Sofia thought about all the adventures they'd had in this beautiful, magical place. She thought about meeting the Shiver Sharks on their first trip, and the surfing seals on their second. She thought about the turtle hatchlings and the smart fish and the narwhals. There were so many amazing creatures that lived in this sea. And the Fire Queen wanted to destroy them all!

The more Sofia thought about it, the more powerful her roar became. The Dragon Girls' combined roars created multicolored bubbles that swirled in the water, so thick that for a moment, they couldn't see anything. But Sofia could hear the furious screeches of the Fire Queen. There was a strange fizzing sound, and suddenly the water felt cooler.

"Stop it!" yelled the Fire Queen, but her voice sounded small and weak.

"It's working!" JellyJo cooed, floating next to Sofia and waving her tentacles excitedly.

Sofia held back her roar for a moment. Grace

and Zoe followed suit. As the bubbles cleared a little, they saw something surprising.

"Am I imagining it, or is the Fire Queen smaller?" Grace asked. She sounded like she could hardly believe it.

"Lies!" screamed the Fire Queen, swimming around in a rage. "Your roars do not affect me at all!"

"She's definitely smaller," Zoe stated. "And she's changing color!"

It was true. Normally, the Fire Queen was so blindingly hot that she looked almost blue. But now the Fire Queen's flaming hair and gown had a red tint. It reminded Sofia of when an open fire was reduced to red embers at the end of the night. She noticed something else, too. Little sparkles were rising from the queen as she swirled and screeched in fury.

"The waterproofing spell she cast over herself must be waning," JellyJo explained. "Your roar weakened her so much that her magic is less powerful."

"Wrong! You'll never destroy me!" the Fire Queen insisted.

But even her sparks were shrinking.

Energy surged through Sofia. It was working! She and her friends roared again. Soon the Fire Queen would vanish forever! But then Sofia had a thought: *Was that really such a good idea?* There were lots of good things about fire after all. Having bonfires on the beach with friends. Cooking over an open flame with her grandpa. And fireworks bursting into the night sky was always a magical sight. Sofia reminded herself that without the fiery power of the sun, life was not possible.

Sofia realized that they did not want the Fire Queen to burn out completely. The queen floated near the three open clamshells. Impulsively, Sofia flipped around and thumped at the water with her tail and wings, whipping up a current. The water surged, catching the queen and making her tumble head over heels. Zoe and Grace stopped roaring when they saw what Sofia was up to.

Soon all three Sea Dragons were working the water with their powerful tails and wings, pushing the Fire Queen closer to the open clamshells.

"Attack them, Fire Sparks!" screamed the queen in her croaky, weak voice.

But it was too late. With one more tail thump, the Sea Dragons sent the Fire Queen tumbling into one of the shells. The shell promptly snapped closed!

For a moment, no one said anything. The Fire Sparks stopped buzzing and everything was still. As they watched, the shell with the Fire Queen inside began to shrink. It became smaller and smaller, until it was no bigger than any ordinary seashell.

The narwhals erupted into loud hoots of joy and clinked horns.

"You did it, Sea Dragons!" Prince Toothy cheered.

Sofia tried to speak, but the cheering noise was so loud she could hardly hear herself, let alone be heard by everyone else.

"Hey," exclaimed Grace, giving Sofia a nudge. "Look who's here!"

Sofia spun around. What she saw made her laugh with delight. The crowd of narwhals had been joined by the Shiver Sharks and the

Diamond Dolphins. Even the laid-back seals who loved surfing had come. The tiny turtles had also arrived, with the Sea Keeper turtle leading the way. The hatchlings clapped their little flippers together and did joyful somersaults when they saw the Sea Dragons.

"How wonderful! But what's going on?" Sofia wondered out loud. "Why is everyone here?"

"They are here because it's time for the Watch Winding ceremony to begin," JellyJo said.

Sofia gasped in alarm. "We have to get to the Undersea Garden! And I don't even know where it is!"

JellyJo pulsed up and down in her gentle, comforting way. "Just wait ... and watch!"

A single ray of moonlight cut through the water, lighting everything up in a calming blue-silver hue.

"The full moon is directly overhead!" Zoe breathed.

Sofia and her friends watched, enchanted.

The cool, silvery light began to spread and broaden. It was like watching curtains opening to reveal a stage.

First, Sofia saw rows of swaying seaweed in many shades of purple and green. Then, as the light swept wider, she saw a pathway lined with bright pink and orange coral plants. In between the coral, golden shells glimmered in the moonlight.

"This is the Undersea Garden!" Grace exclaimed.

Zoe nodded and laughed. "We were right here the whole time," she said. "We just didn't realize."

Sofia was too stunned to speak. It was all so beautiful!

Rising from the center of the Undersea Garden was a white pillar, decorated with shells. Sofia squinted. What was that thing in the middle? It looked a lot like a . . . clock!

Her insides fluttered as JellyJo confirmed what Sofia had just guessed. "That is the Water Watch."

The moonlight shone directly over the watch, making it gleam. It hummed with magical power. Sofia, Zoe, and Grace swam closer so they could see it properly. The watch looked like the kind of old-fashioned one Sofia's grandma wore—only this one was much bigger. It had strange markings around the outside and was transparent, so the Sea Dragons could see the intricate mechanics of the watch. Right in the middle was one small cog that glowed brightly.

Suddenly, the crowd murmured with excitement and parted to let through three figures: a large, wise-looking turtle, a dolphin with a crystal dorsal fin, and Nara the narwhal.

"The Sea Keepers!" Sofia, Grace, and Zoe cheered.

Grasping paws excitedly, the friends looked on as the Sea Keepers approached the Water Watch.

10

The turtle swam to the left of the white pillar,

and the dolphin swam to the right.

In a creaky voice, the turtle began to chant:

"To keep our oceans trouble-free,

this watch is wound by Keepers Three."

Then the dolphin took over in her squeaky voice, with her dorsal fin flashing:

"For all the creatures in the sea,

time will flow for eternity."

A hush fell over the waiting crowd as the narwhal approached the Water Watch. The moonlight lit up Nara, making her horn shine like polished silver. Carefully, she used the tip of her horn to wind the central cog of the Water Watch. The ancient mechanism clicked as it turned.

Sofia and her friends clutched one another. It was working!

Bright, sparkling light burst from the Water Watch, sending gentle ripples through the water. The crowd erupted into cheers of delight.

"The watch has been wound for another year!" JellyJo explained joyfully. "And it's all thanks to you three."

Pride washed over Sofia. She grabbed Grace

and Zoe and wrapped them up in a wing-hug. "We did it! We actually did it!"

"Of course we did." Grace grinned. "We're a great team!"

"The best," Zoe agreed.

"Three cheers for the Sea Dragons!" Toothy called, and the three friends found themselves surrounded by happy sea creatures, all calling their names and patting them on the back with flippers and horns and fish tails.

Sofia wanted this moment to go on forever. There had been some very difficult and scary parts on this quest, but the Sea Dragons had triumphed. It was such a great feeling.

Sofia felt a tap on her shoulder, and, turning,

she saw JellyJo. She knew what her little friend was about to say. "It's time to go, isn't it?"

"I am afraid so," JellyJo said, a little sadly. "The Tree Queen would like to see you before you return home. Bring the shell containing the Fire Queen with you."

Sofia looked at the shrunken clamshell. It was small enough for Sofia to scoop up in one paw. As she did so, she felt the shell of her bracelet give a gentle tug.

Sofia turned to her friends. "My shell will show us the way back to the glade."

The three friends said their goodbyes to the crowd of sea creatures. It was hard to leave them all, especially JellyJo.

"I hope to see you again one day!" Sofia said to her faithful companion as JellyJo wrapped her in her many tentacles.

"I'll be here if you come back!" JellyJo replied, finally releasing Sofia and waving all her tentacles at once.

With powerful flicks of their tails, the three Sea Dragons sped away. They swam side by side through the ocean, until the water became too shallow to swim in. Then they burst out of the water and into the evening sky. Gleaming droplets of water fell from their wings as they took flight.

Up ahead were the tall trees of the Magic Forest, illuminated by the full moon's gentle light. Sofia led the way, guided by the tugging of her bracelet. Word seemed to have spread of the Sea Dragons' success.

Birds called out as the Dragon Girls flew past their nests. Squirrels scampered along branches to watch them pass by.

"Yippee for the Sea Dragons!"

"Well done, Sea Dragons!"

Even the trees themselves seemed to carry a message in the rustling of their leaves. Sofia could have sworn she heard them say, "Thank you. Safe seas mean happy trees!"

By the time the girls arrived at the glade's shimmering barrier, Sofia didn't feel like she was flying at all. It was like floating on pure joy!

She hovered above the force field and turned to her friends. "Ready?"

"Ready!" Zoe and Grace called.

Zoe and Grace dove first. Sofia hovered for a moment, then launched herself down, performing her finest reverse dive yet!

It was bright and cheerful inside the glade. The Tree Queen was waiting for them, a warm smile on her wooden face.

"I couldn't be prouder, Sea Dragons," she said as they approached. "That was a very dangerous and important quest. But together you three achieved everything I asked of you. The Magic Forest—and our seas—will be forever grateful."

"Our pleasure!" Sofia said, nearly bursting

with pride. Then she held out the tiny clam-shell. "We brought you this. The Fire Queen is trapped inside. It didn't feel right to destroy her completely."

The Tree Queen's branches swayed gently as she reached out an arm and took the shell from Sofia. "That was very wise," she said. "Fire is essential. It's only a problem when it gets out of control. I will keep this safe and make sure the Fire Queen never becomes that powerful again."

"So, I guess this is goodbye," Sofia murmured. Glancing at Grace and Zoe, she could see they felt the same way she did. "Should we give back our bracelets?"

The Tree Queen smiled. "No, they are yours to keep, Sea Dragons," she said. "Besides, you will need them for your return home. When you leave the glade, look into your shells. They will show you the way."

With a final shiver of leaves, the queen returned to her tree form.

Sofia, Grace, and Zoe hugged. "See you back at the lagoon!" Sofia called. With a last glance around the glade, the three friends flew up and out of the shimmering force field and into the cool evening air.

Sofia looked at her shell as the Tree Queen had instructed. In the center was a tiny image of a lagoon. As Sofia watched, the image grew larger and larger. It merged with the night sky, and soon Sofia could not tell what was water and what was air.

Closing her eyes, she tucked her wings tightly to her body and dove ...

When Sofia opened her eyes, she was float-ing in water. But she knew she was no longer in the Magic Forest. She was back in the lagoon near camp! She stretched her arms up. Yes, they were the perfectly ordinary arms of a girl once again. It was amazing being a dragon, but as Sofia looked around, she couldn't be sad about being back. The surface of the water was a mass of oranges and pinks, reflecting the setting sun.

"Sofia! Over here!"

Two figures were leaping up and down on the shore, waving. Grace and Zoe were no longer in dragon form, but they looked every bit as happy as they had in the Magic Forest.

On the beach behind them, the counselors had built a giant bonfire.

"Come and join us!" her friends called. "We're going to toast marshmallows."

"Coming!" Sofia called as she swam to shore.

It had been an incredible adventure—one she would never, ever forget. But being back here with her camp friends was also wonderful. And she intended to enjoy every last moment.

Another magical series from Maddy Mara!

Turn the page for a special sneak peek of

THE SPROUT FAIRIES

Forever Fairies

Lulu, Coco, Nova, and Zali clustered around the bigger fairy. They all began talking at once.

"Hi! What's your name?"

"What do we do next?"

"How did you know we were here?"

"Are we going to fly somewhere?"

The bigger fairy put up her hands and

laughed. "Slow down, Sprouties! You'll find out much more if you let me speak."

The little fairies fell silent. Their wings shimmered in the morning light.

"My name is Etta," said the fairy, flicking back her ponytail. "And I'm here to bring you to the Forever Tree."

Lulu's daffodil had told her about the Forever Tree. The Forever Fairies all lived within its branches. Lulu could hardly wait to see it!

The Sprout Wings had a thousand more questions.

"How far away is it?"

"Do you live there?"

"What happens when we arrive?"

"Can we go there right now?"

Etta laughed again, shaking her head in wonder. "You are the most excited Sprouties I've ever met. I'll explain on the way. But first, zip over to those white flowers and back. We have a long journey ahead. I need to see how well you can fly."

The four little fairies fluttered across the glade toward the white flowers. Lulu was in front. She just loved flying! With each flap of her wings, she surged through the air, faster and faster.

As Lulu neared the white flowers, she saw a bug sparkling in the sunlight—and it was about to fall off a petal! Lulu swooshed over and caught the bug in her arms. "I've got you!" She popped it safely onto a bigger petal and kept flying. Lulu was going so fast she almost crashed into Coco, Nova, and Zali coming the other way. "Sorry!" she called.

"Wow! You're so speedy!" Nova said.

"Wait for us!" Coco laughed.

Lulu hadn't realized how far ahead she was. The funny thing was, she didn't feel like she'd been trying very hard.

When Lulu returned, Etta smiled. "Good flying. And that was a nice rescue. Sparklebugs can be so clumsy! Let me guess, you had lots of flying dreams when you were growing in your flower?"

"I did!" Lulu said. "But it's even better in real life."

Etta nodded. "You and I are alike."

Lulu beamed. She loved the idea of being like this fast, cool fairy.

Soon, Nova, Coco, and Zali joined them, panting but happy.

"Was that okay?" Zali puffed. "We're not as fast as Lulu. She's amazing!"

Lulu felt a flash of worry. Should she have slowed down? She didn't want the others to think she was showing off. She already liked the other Sprout Wings, and she wanted them to like her back!

"You all did wonderfully," Etta said. "Sprouties

usually take a while to get the hang of flying. But you four are naturals."

"Shall we go?" Coco asked. "I can't wait to see the Forever Tree."

"I like your enthusiasm, Coco. Yes, let's go!" Etta turned and headed for the dense thicket surrounding the glade. Coco, Nova, and Zali followed close behind.

Lulu turned to look at her daffodil one last time. It gave a bob of its yellow head. "Safe travels, Lulu. I know you'll make me proud!"

Lulu waved goodbye and sped off after the others. She caught up easily.

Etta spoke as they flew over a grove of wildflowers. "The Forever Fairies protect the forest in lots of different ways. We've done this forever—and we'll keep doing it forever! Even the oldest creatures of the forest cannot remember a time when we weren't here, helping out."

Nova looked curious. "How do we look after the forest?"

"That depends on which pod you're put into," Etta said.

"Ooh! My flower told me about the fairy pods," Coco said. "There are four different ones, right?"

"That's correct," Etta said. "There are the Flutterflies, that's my pod. Then there are the Shimmerbuds, Twinklestars, and Sparkleberries. Over the next few days, you will do a series of tryouts to discover which pod you each belong in."

Coco clapped, excited. "What do we have to do for these tryouts?"

Nova looked calm and thoughtful. "Will we be given time to practice?".

Zali was gazing off dreamily. "What's it like, being in Flutterfly?"

Lulu had a question, too. It was a big one: Could all four Sprout Wings be in the same pod?

But before Lulu could ask anything, Etta called, "Watch out, everyone!"

Etta ducked under the low-hanging branch that had appeared. Lulu did the same, followed by Coco. Nova approached next, swooping under the branch in her careful way. Lulu looked around for Zali. She was trailing behind the group, gazing around in wonder. She clearly hadn't heard Etta's warning.

In a flash, Lulu zoomed back to the tiny fairy. She grabbed Zali's hand and pulled her under the branch just in time.

"Whoops!" Zali looked frazzled. "Thanks, Lulu!"

Etta nodded at them approvingly. "It's good that you're watching out for your fellow Sprouties, Lulu."

Lulu felt a glow of pride.

They were deep in the forest now, flying between huge, mossy trees. Beams of sunshine filtered through the canopy. Lulu felt like she could fly forever. But then she glanced at the others. Nova's wings were looking a little droopy. So were Coco's and Zali's.

I'll help them out, Lulu decided. She looped up and over the group so that she was behind them. She started flapping the air with her wings to push the other fairies along. But instead of helping, Lulu's gusts of wind tossed the little fairies in all directions. Nova's hat got caught in Zali's long hair, and Coco was flipped upside down.

"Oops! Sorry!" cried Lulu.

But everyone just laughed as they straightened themselves out.

"That was a good thought, Lulu," Etta said. "The Turbo Boost is a very complex Flutterfly move, and you nearly nailed it. I'll teach you how to perfect it someday. But don't worry, we're almost at the tree now. We just need to get through those brambles."

Up ahead was a twisted snarl of vines studded with thorns. Lulu could just make out a few narrow tunnels through the tangle.

"Follow me," Etta called cheerfully. "But don't get hooked on the thorns!" She disappeared into the brambles. After a moment's hesitation, Coco followed.

"Here goes," muttered Nova, flying through a little slower.

Lulu knew she could zip through the brambles easily. But then she looked at Zali. Her face was very pale.

"Let's go through together," Lulu suggested.

Linking arms, the two fairies squeezed through the gap, nipping under one vine and around another, avoiding all the sharp thorns.

A moment later, Lulu and Zali burst through the brambles. Waiting for them on the other side was the most incredible sight.

An enormous tree loomed before them. Its mossy trunk was as wide as three normal trees. It was so tall, Lulu couldn't see the top! Countless little windows were dotted along the sturdy branches. At the base of the trunk was a grand door, golden and etched with swirling patterns.

Lulu gasped. "The Forever Tree!"

"It's just how I imagined." Coco sighed.

Nova nodded, her eyes sparkling. Zali simply stared.

As they watched, the Forever Tree gave a dramatic shake . . . and burst into bloom! In an instant, the branches were covered in flowers of every color imaginable.

"Come on, Sprouties!" Etta cried, hovering near the huge trunk. "The other fairies are waiting."

The four Sprout Wings looked at one another, confused. What other fairies?

There was the sound of tinkling bells and the front door flung open. A stream of fairies poured out and surged into the air, cheering loudly. More fairies squeezed out of the windows, flitting here and there in the golden sunlight.

There were boy fairies and girl fairies, tall fairies and short fairies. Fairies with long raven-black hair and fairies with short purple hair. Some of the fairies were around Etta's age, and others were only a bit bigger than the Sprout Wings. All the fairies were dressed in colorful outfits. And all of them were chattering with excitement.

"The new Sprouties are here!"

"Look how cute they are!"

"So tiny! They still have pollen on their wings."

Etta flew to the front of the crowd. "Flutter back, everyone!" Her voice rang out clear and firm. "Give our new Sprout Wings some space. Remember what it felt like on your first day."

ABOUT THE AUTHORS

Maddy Mara is the pen name of Australian creative duo Hilary Rogers and Meredith Badger. Hilary and Meredith have been making children's books together for many years. They love dreaming up new ideas and always have lots of projects bubbling away. When not writing, Hilary can be found cooking weird things or going on long walks, often with Meredith. And Meredith can be found teaching English online all around the world or daydreaming about being able to fly. They both currently live in Melbourne, Australia. Their website is maddymara.com.

DRAGON GAMES

PLAY THE GAME. SAVE THE REALM.

DRAGON GIRLS

**#1: Azmina the Gold
Glitter Dragon**

**#2: Willa the Silver
Glitter Dragon**

**#3: Naomi the Rainbow
Glitter Dragon**

**#4: Mei the Ruby
Treasure Dragon**

**#5: Aisha the Sapphire
Treasure Dragon**

**#6: Quinn the Jade
Treasure Dragon**

**#7: Rosie the
Twilight Dragon**

**#8: Phoebe the
Moonlight Dragon**

**#9: Stella the
Starlight Dragon**

**#10: Grace the
Cove Dragon**

**#11: Zoe the
Beach Dragon**

**#12: Sofia the
Lagoon Dragon**

Collect them all!